Moses Lewis Scudder

Congested Prices

Moses Lewis Scudder

Congested Prices

Reprint of the original, first published in 1883.

1st Edition 2024 | ISBN: 978-3-38533-014-6

Verlag (Publisher): Outlook Verlag GmbH, Zeilweg 44, 60439 Frankfurt, Deutschland
Vertretungsberechtigt (Authorized to represent): E. Roepke, Zeilweg 44, 60439 Frankfurt, Deutschland
Druck (Print): Books on Demand GmbH, In de Tarpen 42, 22848 Norderstedt, Deutschland

CONGESTED PRICES.

By M. L. SCUDDER, Jr.

CHICAGO:
JANSEN, McCLURG & COMPANY.
1883.

CONGESTED PRICES.

By the title "Congested Prices," I intend to describe prices made in certain unhealthy conditions of trade. There are times in the existence of our best organized commercial systems when the streams of exchanges, usually flowing quietly and evenly, become clogged by mad rushes. At such times, like the agitated blood in the human body under abnormal conditions, the excited efforts to effect transfers of property become too strong for the customary channels. There is a heaping up, a congestion of prices at weak points, and, unless speedy relief is afforded, the prostration or destruction of the commercial system follows.

As the knowledge of the cause and cure of disease is the proper direction in which to seek the preservation of health, so the study of the nature of commercial crises is the best method of preserving a sound condition of trade. For this reason the investigation of prices in a state of congestion leads to the prevention of panics, and cultivates that intelligent and sober state of mind which confines business ventures within prudent limits.

It may be noted in the outset that the subject of prices is largely within the bounds of mental science. The desire for possession, the comparison of desires, the fear

of deprivation, the far-reaching effort to apprehend by
analogy the desires of others — all these mental phenomena are manifested in the making of prices, and,
political economists to the contrary notwithstanding,
are better worth investigating than the amount of labor
expended in production or the extent of the wage-fund.

Prices are values expressed in money terms; but there
is also, I think, a more restricted meaning to the term
in common commercial use which is not noted in the
dictionaries. Price, I think, implies that a transaction
has actually been effected ; at least this is true in markets
where transactions are effected by offerings and bids. A
merchant may mark the prices on his goods at which he
hopes to make sales, but a dealer in grain, provisions or
stocks would hardly make use of the term in the same
way in regard to his commodities. He might possibly
speak of it as the "seller's price," but the word price
alone would mean for him only the money value of a
commodity as determined by an actual transaction.
This distinction is important. There are in common
use the terms "bidding price" and "asking price," but
neither is regarded as the real price established by an
actual exchange.

With this meaning clearly understood, the term "con-
jested prices" becomes more significant, and the importance of mental conditions is more definitely brought
out. The opinions of men, their desires, their needs,
are the elements to be studied. How comes it that for
long periods, by diligent comparison of their multiform

wants and wishes, having succeeded in accomplishing
by exchange a very satisfactory state of existence, men
all at once unite in desiring one thing intently, and
direct all their efforts, without consideration or judgment, to attaining it? This is the problem of panics.
On September 23, 1873, spring wheat sold in Chicago
at 1.04½ per bushel; on September 24 it sold at 89
cents per bushel. Why was this sudden change in its
value? Political economists assure us that value is determined by cost of production. Yet we are quite sure
there was no great change in the cost of production of
wheat within these twenty-four hours. The reason for
the decline is to be found in the opinions and desires
of men, and the laws of the opinions and desires of men
are the chief laws of prices.

It must be conceded that this subject hardly admits
of logical treatment. The data are so widely scattered,
so numerous and so minute, that their classification in
anything like a connected theory is impossible. One
in treating this subject conscientiously can only pick up
an interesting fact here and another there, point out the
peculiarities of each and cast them away again. If these
observations seem to teach any valuable lesson, it must
come from a previous mental agreement between listener
and speaker, for there is no well placed solid foundation
amongst these facts upon which a reasoner can build so
as to command the agreement of all mankind.

From the ungraspable nature of this subject, it is at
once the easiest and the most difficult to treat. The

easiest, if one is willing to dogmatize or to prophesy, for in this uncertain field a dogmatic assertion or a prophecy may possibly prove correct ; but the most difficult, if one sincerely and by sound method strives to reach a positive conclusion. The effort to compass and comprehend the infinite number of facts is as yet too great for the mind. We cannot get a satisfactory hold on the particulars which will warrant us in working up surely to the general law.

In the mechanism of prices, stock and grain exchanges have prominent places. They are organizations for the chief purpose of determining and recording prices. They are developments from the demands of trade, but not the less is the ingenuity remarkable which has constructed them and fitted them with well established customs and carefully drawn rules, so that prices with uniform conditions are made momentarily, hourly, daily, for the guidance of all the trading world. The advantage of prices made on these exchanges is their mathematical certainty. Compared with outside trading they are as the demonstrations of Euclid to practical surveying. They have a certain quality of abstractness, which makes one inclined to call them " pure prices."

These exchanges are undoubtedly the developments of the fairs of the middle ages. But they have totally changed their characters. The merchants and farmers who attended the fairs of Stourbridge or Winchester brought their goods and produce, made their exchanges and took away their purchases. But a very small percentage of those who buy or sell on the exchanges of the great commercial centers desire to possess the property which they purchase, or are in possession of the property which they sell. The fixing of the price is the main object of nearly all transactions on these exchanges. For every transaction there must be a purchaser and a seller, and the price once fixed is made the basis of a contract. To the fixing of this price each party to the contract brings his widest information and his best judgment. One of the two parties must be in error in his judgment, as to the supply of, or the demand for, the commodity concerning which they contract. In the course of time it is apparent on which side the error of judgment has been made. But it rarely happens that either party waits for the other to complete his contract. The loser takes his loss when he pleases by making another contract for the purchase or sale of the same commodity with another party, and the winner takes his profit in the same way. It is customary to set off one contract against another. Thus there are always a large number of contracts always in existence between the members of every exchange, and these contracts are almost always for a very much larger quantity of commodity traded in than is in existence within easy reach of the contracting parties.

This is roughly the method by which these great exchanges are conducted. It is not strictly accurate as to the details, for every commodity is subject to peculiar conditions, and it is a recognized principle of all exchanges that delivery and payment, according to the terms of the contract, must be rigidly enforced if either party desires it. If it were not for this principle the prices made on the various exchanges would be without value to commerce ; with this principle they become the guide of all transactions within the civilized world.

I wish here to bring out prominently this point, that these exchanges and boards of trade are mainly occupied in determining prices. It is a sort of division of labor. The members of these exchanges are not greatly employed in handling or using the commodities whose prices they develop. Their business is to determine the prices, and in the economy of employments it falls to others to possess and enjoy the property.

It is not to be understood that the members of any of the prominent exchanges determine prices solely according to their own desires. Every such exchange is the center of general attention ; many thousands of interested men are listening to the click of the telegraph instruments which report its doings, and every quotation made is the result of innumerable and widespread influences, as far beyond the control of a board of brokers as are the clouds or the seasons.

It is hardly worth while to discuss here the morality of speculation in the various exchanges. That is a subject very much misunderstood, and neither the opinions of learned judges nor the statutes of Illinois have served to make it plainer ; but, whether it is right or wrong, it is certainly the height of folly for an excitable or inexperienced person, with a small margin, thus to attempt to take a hand in fixing the price of an important commodity.

It is true, however, that this kind of speculation performs an important office for trade and commerce,— a part in the machinery of the world's business which cannot be abolished, any more than the railroads can be done away with because the locomotive occasionally slaughters a careless citizen.

Very few persons were ruined financially by speculation in wheat before the days of trading in futures, of negotiable warehouse receipts, and of the labor-saving machinery of the board of trade. When it was necessary to pay in full out of one's capital for every bushel of grain bought, to provide a place to store it, and to go to all the trouble of receiving and keeping it, taking a flyer in wheat was no easy matter, and persons of inadequate means did not often engage in that amusement. Now it is the improvement of the machinery—the greater momentum of which it is capable—which makes it tempting, and which also makes it dangerous. The old-fashioned carpenter's saw rarely maimed or injured the boys and careless working-men who handled it, but the modern buzz-saw, which now does nearly all the work of the older instrument with twenty times the speed and economy, cuts off fingers and thumbs, and otherwise frequently lacerates heedless persons who meddle with it. It is as much more dangerous as it is more efficient. Yet no one thinks of

denouncing the buzz-saw for the lost fingers and
thumbs, or advocating its destruction.   The machinery
of the Board of Trade is only a big commercial buzz-
saw.   By its means more exchanges are made in a day
than fifty years ago could be made in a year, yet it will
sometimes amputate a bank account or lacerate a
fortune before a careless speculator knows he is hurt.
But we should not, therefore, condemn the Board of
Trade.

It is best to explain that nearly all dealings on the New
York Stock Exchange are invariably settled by delivery
and payment, and that sales there for future delivery
are insignificant in amount.   In almost all transactions
the stocks or securities bought are delivered and paid
for on the following day.   There are there no regular
settling days, when accounts are adjusted against each
other, as on the Stock Exchange in London or on the
Paris Bourse, or in all the grain and cotton exchanges.
The New York stock brokers are enabled, by means of
the large amount of banking and other loanable funds
which their business has attracted to Wall street, to borrow money on the stocks and securities, in which they
deal, to make their payments in full every day.   To
this fact, I think, is to be attributed a part of the great
influence which the New York Stock Exchange exercises in the commercial affairs of the country.   It not
only determines the prices of the chief of those investments in which the fixed capital of the country is engaged, but it also exhibits the rate at which the loanable

funds of the country are to a great extent employed. This is no insignificant influence. In the study of prices it is very important, and it gives to the quotations and operations of the New York Stock Exchange a paramount and commanding position in the financial affairs of this land. It is the fashion with many editors and demagogues to denounce the stock "gambling of Wall street," and they doubtless lead many ignorant persons to believe that the Stock Exchange is a disreputable and harmful spot, that the world would be better without it. I think that a careful examination of its office and influence, its methods and character, will prove it to be a highly beneficial and well managed institution.

The reports of the Comptroller of the Currency show that forty per cent of the loans of the national banks of New York city are demand loans on stock collateral, and presumably for Stock Exchange business. It is estimated, by the same authority, that about forty-six per cent of the business of the banks in the clearing-house in New York city is for transactions on the Stock Exchange, and the clearings of these banks are seventy-six per cent of those of the whole country.

It is easy to see, from these figures, that no other single organization exercises an influence equal to that of the New York Stock Exchange upon the financial affairs of the United states. Indeed no line of trade or manufactures, nor any combination of them that is likely to be made, can equal its influence.

I have endeavored to make plain these few points concerning the use, character and importance of exchanges, because it is now chiefly in the quotations made on these exchanges that we must study prices. The great agricultural products are now bought and sold exclusively on exchange quotations, and no one is more benefited by this machinery than the farmer. He is able to know, with considerable precision, what his product is worth at the time he offers it for sale.. The value of that knowledge to him can hardly be over-estimated. He would otherwise be at the mercy of middlemen and speculators.

The efficiency of these exchanges has developed rapidly in recent years, under the influence of rapid transportation and the development of the telegraph system. There is nothing in civilization more wonderful than the machinery by which prices are made and reported to every part of the world.

It is by the study of the prices made by the great exchanges that we can today best learn the workings of the laws of trade. We have, as it were, in a microcosm, the opinion of all interested persons as to the money value of the chief articles of commerce at each particular moment of each business day.

It is probable, too, that the modern improvements have considerably modified the fluctuations in prices.

In the development through the ages of the influence of prices upon human affairs certain cities stand out as focal points from which that influence has radiated —

Sidon, Tyre and Carthage, Athens and Corinth, Venice
and Genoa, then Amsterdam, and now London, to be
followed by New York, perhaps, before the world is a
hundred years older. There are a thousand cities on
the globe more prosperous than ancient Sidon ever was,
but there are none which have been of greater benefit to
man. The Phœnician galleys, coasting the shores of
the Mediterranean, were first to show that the wants of
mankind can be better satisfied by agreement than by
force. It was a new principle that bargaining may
create power; that exchanges in which each party gains
are surer to secure riches than robbery. We know very
little of the life at Sidon. Very likely the Sidonians
began business as pirates, but found trading more
profitable. They are entitled to credit for the dis-
covery. The fact that they were known as Sidonians
rather than the subjects of any king speaks well for
them. It indicates some idea of equality in citizenship,
a well-defined notion of individual right of property,
and a government by common consent. Tyre and
Carthage preserved this characteristic, and indeed
through the centuries, from that time, cities of commercial importance have been greater than their rulers.
Unlimited kingship has invariably destroyed commercial
prosperity. It is essential to commercial prosperity
that buyer and seller can meet on terms of commercial equality; that they can be free to consult their
own interests only, and to trade or not to trade, as
seems best to them. It is only under such circumstances
that fair prices can be made; and this is the reason why

the great commercial cities of the world have been free cities. Whether the desire for a fair bargain preceded the desire for civil freedom, no one can tell, but the ideas could not have been far apart. And we may conclude that the Sidonian merchants, shrouded for us in anti-Homeric gloom, carrying out their purple robes, and bringing back Eyptian corn and Spanish iron, wine from Cyprus and gold from Lydia, were the first practical advocates of liberty, as they were the first instructors of mankind in the art of acquiring riches by voluntary exchange.

Fair prices can only be made where buyer and seller meet on terms of perfect commercial equality. There must be equal freedom to trade or not to trade for all parties to transactions. We can imagine a highwayman taking a thousand dollars from his victim and leaving his old hat in exchange, but we would hardly say that the price of the hat was a thousand dollars. The exchanges of property among savage tribes are often of this unfair character ; so also is much of the commerce under despotic governments. The trading in the bazaars of Central Asia at the present time is largely of this nature. The leader of a tribe of Turcomans can secure much more favorable bargains than he who has no armed horsemen at his command, for there is a probability that the chief will take by force what he wants if the price does not suit him.

It is not absolutely certain that this element of in-timidation is absent from all the transactions of civilized life. One party to a transaction may so threaten the other as to force his acceptance of unsatisfactory terms. Such transactions are void in law, but sometimes the law cannot be successfully applied. In such cases no fair price is made.

I think also that something of this unfairness is considered to exist, when sales or purchases are made under compulsion of law or of rules of trade. For example, prices made in judicial sales are not regarded as strictly fair, nor are those made to enforce defaulted contracts under the regulations of boards of trade. The persons for whose account such transactions are made may have no right to object, but as they have no voluntary part in fixing the prices, such prices are not regarded as fairly quotable in establishing actual value.

There is a certain analogy between the weather and prices. To be sure the phenomena of the weather are natural, while the phenomena of prices are the creations of man ; but these phenomena are equally beyond man's intelligent control as yet, and perhaps equally influence his welfare.

It is interesting to trace the growth of the fabric of prices from the earliest rude exchanges of property to the present intricate network of financial relations, which pervades civilization like an atmosphere, sustaining all commercial life, and making possible the enlightened comfort and happiness of the race. It is hardly possible to gain an adequate conception of the change in the condition of man through the development of

2

the system of prices. We may compare Abraham in the first recorded monetary transaction, buying the field of Ephron for four hundred shekels of silver "current money of the merchants," with his latest descendants, the Rothschilds, bringing the enterprises of nations and of kings to the tribunal of the money market. The prices of corn and mutton were matters of small concern to the men of Abraham's day. They made their own arrangements for food independent of their neighbors' wants. They planted their fields and tended their flocks and defended them, and, according to their success in these pursuits, did they and their children have much or little to eat. But now, in Rothschild's time, each minute want of Jew and Gentile is conceived of on a money scale. It is attainable or impossible according to its price. Almost every action of a very large part of mankind is controlled by considerations of price.

In Abraham's time, and for many hundred years afterward, rulers and warriors and priests, governments and armies and religions were entirely independent of prices, but the meshes gradually tightened round them, and now there is no potentate or statesman or pope who dares to disregard the market. There is no government foolish enough to move against the current of prices, no army can make headway against it, and religions are contented to go along with it.

There is a certain analogy, as I have said, between the weather and prices. Somewhat the same qualities, of mind and disposition, which make the weather-wise man also make the market-wise man. Much watching of the clouds and much experience of storms create the instinct which forewarns changes. Much buying and selling, long observance of demand and production, one or two practical trials of a panic, produce a sense of commercial fluctuation.

The price prophet, like the weather prophet, rarely is able to give satisfactory reasons for his opinions, yet he is equally confident of his own infallibility. The price prophet, like the weather prophet, if successful, has a following of blind and wondering disciples.

The attempt to discover a science of prices is also like the attempt to formulate a science of the weather in a condition of uncertainty. Each science is sought in a series of averages, and each has progressed only so far as to offer to the curious observer long tables of figures and mathematical charts of differences, from which he can draw only vague conclusions. If there is to be a science of prices it must be developed, like meteorology, through the classification of the records of innumerable observations.

It may be interesting to note in this connection the singular superstitions and the absurd theories which, to a considerable extent, influence the actions of men with reference to prices, and which resemble nothing so closely as the old wife superstitions and maxims of sailors and farmers concerning weather. Many specula-lators are governed in their operations by the conviction

that prices decline on Friday more often than on any
other day of the week.   I know a man who prefers to
buy stocks on Tuesday.   Many pious people pray for
higher prices of property which they wish to sell.   I
have heard of a grain speculator, who requested the
prayers of his minister to enable him to sell at a profitable advance, and who vowed to give a considerable
sum to a religious charity if Providence favored his
petition.   There is a very general feeling among business men that their individual luck controls prices.
Some say, "If I buy, prices will be sure to decline; if I
sell, they will be sure to advance."   This is like the
common notion of an individual that his carrying an
umbrella will prevent rain, or his leaving his umbrella
at home will bring on a shower.

Hardly any trader is free from some sort of fetichism
in his dealing.   Good or bad luck is believed to be
associated with various inanimate objects.   As storms
are supposed by sailors to follow a certain ship, so mis-
fortune is thought to dwell in certain shops.   I have
heard of an operator on the Board of Trade grinding
to pieces under his feet the lead pencil which has
recorded losing transactions.

Another similarity between the market and the
weather is the tendency which we have to personify
them.   We know that each atmospheric change is produced by many causes, and also that each fluctuation of
prices depends on numerous special reasons.   Yet we
disregard and seemingly forget these facts in thinking

or speaking of them. We conceive of them as we would of an army moving under one leadership. We say of the weather, it rains or it is warm, as we say of the market, it rises or it is strong. Changes of prices are the results of the comparisons of innumerable opinions, but we see only the aggregate and forget the individuals which make it.

We talk of the irresistible laws of trade, of prices or of credit, and yet we believe in man's free agency. We surely believe that each transaction in trade is an act of voluntary judgment, and yet we treat these transactions in the aggregate as if they were predestined and unavoidable.

Tracing the analogy between the weather and prices, it will be observed that men show a tendency to arrange the phenomena of each in cycles, and by noting the succession of events in the past to predict the same successions in the future. There is something in the idea of a cycle which is peculiarly attractive to the mind. It is more satisfactory to describe life by a graceful, well rounded curve, than by a line which is jagged and incomplete. This is shown in all fields of inquiry. We search history for curves of conduct, and, when we find them, make them conspicuous, and we will generally allow ourselves to patch up our favorite curves in their faulty parts at the expense of fidelity to facts. It is our disposition to believe in heroes, who did no wrong, and in villains who showed no good qualities, and to expect that history will repeat itself.

So the weather prophet, anxious to satisfy the human craving for a curve, arranges meteorological events in cycles, and endeavors to show, because cold and heat, rain and snow, frost and drought, have occurred in a certain order in the past, that this same order constitutes a natural law, and will be followed in the future.   I am not intimately acquainted with the methods of the eminent weather prophets.   Indeed they and "their little systems have their days and cease to be" so rapidly, that one hardly has time to give his unreserved adherence to any of them before the failure of some unlucky prophecy consigns the prophet and his system to oblivion.   But I have observed that the cycle theory is accepted by all, as if it were a scientific fact, and the only difficulty is supposed to be in describing the cycle correctly.

These remarks apply only to the long-range weather prophets, who endeavor to map out the weather of a season in advance, and not to the painstaking signal-service observers, whose best hope is to be correct, twice out of three times, in locating a storm after it has begun.

There is no bureau of government for the observation and foretelling of prices.   But there are conscious and unconscious price prophets throughout the country in great numbers, and I think that the belief in the cycle theory of prices is almost universal.

It will not do to treat this theory with disrespect.   It has been favorably considered by the most eminent English writers on this subject.   It is the opinion of Tooke and Newmarch, of Bagehot and Giffen, that there are such cycles. But none of these writers attempt to give the law by which such cycles may be foretold, or do more than point out, with great shrewdness and accuracy, some of the facts which have attended the rising and falling of prices in the past. I think that the use of the term cycle by these authorities is misleading. It is properly to be applied to the recurrence of a certain order of events at a certain period. The element of time is essential to the idea of a cycle, and if the same events recur even in the same order, but at varying times, there is no cycle shown.

It cannot be denied that the course of prices can be approximately represented by curved lines. But the fascinating idea that it can be represented by a regular recurring curve, that is by a cyclical curve, is quite another matter.

I think, however, that this idea quite generally prevails among men who are in the habit of reasoning upon the course of prices, and vague beliefs are common that certain years, at set intervals from past financial crises, will witness future panics and general liquidations.

The most consistent attempt, which I have met with, to mark these years down definitely in the calendar is the work of an Ohio farmer named Benner. He published a small book in 1876 called "Benner's Prophecies," which passed through several editions, and is still read with attention and belief. It is a most curious volume, not only on account of the definiteness with which some of the prophecies have thus far been fulfilled, but also as an illustration of the kind of rea-

soning upon which general prophecies concerning prices
and weather depend. Farmer Benner was a positive
man. His prophecies must have been compiled in
1874 and 1875. His most positive declarations are concerning prices of pig-iron and hogs, and concerning
the next period of general commercial and financial
disaster. As to prices of pig-iron from 1875 to 1882,
his prophecies have been in a measure fulfilled. He said
that pig-iron would sell lowest in 1877, would begin
advancing in 1878, and that its price would culminate
in 1881, and that it would then decline again, reaching
its lowest point once more in 1888. These predictions
so far have been justified by events, and judging from
them alone we are disposed to give farmer Benner great
glory. But when we examine his forecastings as to the
prices of hogs we do not find him so fortunate. According to his ·cycles in the hog trade, prices were to
be highest in 1875, would decline in 1876, and reach
lowest figures in 1877; would rise during 1878 and
1879 and would culminate in 1880. They would decline again in 1881 and reach the lowest point in 1883,
etc. The facts are that hogs sold as high in 1876 as
in 1875, were lower in 1877, but not so low as in 1878
and 1879. They sold as a rule higher in 1881 than in
1880, and were higher still in 1882. Not one of Benner's prophecies concerning the prices of hogs has been
fulfilled. But it is much more remarkable that anyone
should correctly foretell the course of prices of pig-
iron than that anyone should fail to foretell the prices
of hogs. For this reason I have tried to discover upon

what principle farmer Benner proceeded in reaching his conclusions. But, like all other prophets, he can only inadequately explain his system; but as far as he explains it, it is arithmetical, and consists simply in ascertaining the general course of the price of any important commodity in the past and predicting the same fluctuations for the same length of time in the future. For example, concerning the periods of commercial prosperity in this country, he finds that there were panics followed by general liquidations in 1819, 1837, 1857 and 1873. He assumes that the interval from 1819 to 1873, fifty-four years, constitutes a cyclical period, and that within this period are three smaller cycles of eighteen, twenty and sixteen years respectively, corresponding to the intervals between the several panics. He assumes that a new cyclical period of fifty-four years began after 1873, and that the first small cycle of eighteen years will end in 1891, for which year, accordingly, he predicts a great financial revulsion. This is the only substantial basis on which these prophecies rest, and this is sufficiently inconclusive; and yet I think that this reasoning fairly represents the popular theory of high and low prices.

Farmer Benner is plainly not entirely satisfied with the logical character of his system, for he continually breaks the thread of his argument with sententious advice to his fellow men and with proverbs of his own coining, and these are only another illustration that the same mental qualities characterize the weather prophet and the price prophet. And, as if to complete the analogy, farmer Benner concludes his treatise by claiming that

"the cause producing the periodicity and length of
these cycles may be found in our solar system," and
then goes on to treat vaguely of meteorological cycles
and planetary equinoxes, with very much the same air
of mystical wisdom with which Tice and Vennor and
Wiggins and others discourse of the causes and periodicity of storms.

It seems hardly necessary to produce evidence in op-
position to the cycle theory of prices after this example
of its last analysis.   But there is, I believe, a general
belief in it.   The expression, "a panic is not due yet,"
is often heard, and the larger part of the public rest in
the conviction that a commercial revulsion, like an
eclipse of the sun, can be calculated and foretold if only
the proper persons are awake to their duty.

After witnessing the panic of September, 1873, from
the gallery of the Stock Exchange in New York, the
editor of the *Nation* comforted his readers with the
assurance that panics occur in England once in ten
years, and in this country once in twenty years, and
concludes with these words: " If this theory be correct,
our next great panic will be due about 1877.   Let us
hope, however, that the present slight attack may inspire
enough prudence and good sense to ward it off."   This
is the astronomer so distracted by his calculation, that
he doesn't know a total eclipse, even when the umbra
covers him.

A careful account of all the great revulsions in prices,

I think, will show that no one has been a repetition of others. Each has had its peculiar characteristics and causes.

But this opens the field for history into which I cannot enter. The stories of the great panics have been fully and accurately told by many able writers. A reading of them will show that great panics are as dissimilar as great battles. We can acquire from them no more reason for concluding that we will experience a financial panic once in ten or twenty years than from the facts of military history that we shall pass through a great war once in so often.

In this country the panic of 1837 was precipitated by wild speculation in land, and that of 1857 by unsound banking. In England the panic of 1846 was brought about by unwarranted expenditure in railroad building ; that of 1866 by too great confidence in limited liability companies.

The panic of 1873 was caused by over speculation in all commercial countries. Robert Giffen, the present President of the London Statistical Society, looking at it from an English standpoint, called it a " foreign-loans panic." From an American standpoint, it was a general-loan panic. The American people generally had borrowed money and bought property. Real estate, not only in the west, but in the cities and towns of the east, was largely mortgaged. Railroads were mortgages to a greater extent probably, in proportion to their cost, than any other kind of property. Manufacturing companies carried heavy bonded debts and heavy lines of discount.   Merchants had all the paper out which the banks and their friends would take.

Former panics in this country had been greatly influenced by distrust of the currency.   There was nothing of this in 1873.   Men hoarded greenbacks and national bank notes with absolute confidence in their value.

Former panics have been created to some extent by special disasters, such as deficient harvests or wars or political commotions.   There were none of these in 1873.   Crops were abundant, and the world was at peace.

It was simply a realization on the part of a great number of men that they had borrowed more than they could readily pay, or that they had lent more than they could readily collect.   The business of the country was done on a too narrow margin of capital.   The suspension of the house of Jay Cooke & Co., the closing of the New York Stock Exchange, the suspensions which followed, the devices of the banks to resist the first rush of excited depositors—these were but the striking incidents which were not especially characteristic of the course of events.   But the gradual liquidations which followed, with gradually declining prices through several years, are peculiar and noteworthy.   This decline was resisted by strenuous arguments, and by mutual assurances of confidence.   But those who sold their properties at once and settled their accounts, were the most fortunate.   These were few.   Nearly all masked their eagerness to sell behind declarations that the decline in prices was but a temporary reaction, that prices would soon improve, and that properties were cheap. And thus the long and weary struggle went on, between growing interest accounts and maturing loans on one side, and shrinking assets and decreasing incomes on the other, until it ended for many in bankruptcy, disgrace and poverty. Lenders suffered as greatly as borrowers. Indeed, it was impossible to classify the people in this way, for the majority of business men were both borrowers and lenders. Lenders were compelled to take collateral and securities which they did not want and could not use, and which they in their turn sacrificed at the first opportunity.

There was nothing especially calculated to give warning of approaching disaster in the course of events just before the panic of 1873. The daily record of financial matters during the summer of 1873 reads like the story of greatest confidence and security. In August the stock market was dull, with good prices for leading stocks. Money was easy, and the banks held reserves largely in excess of the legal requirement. Early in September Mr. Jay Gould was credited with an attempt to run a corner in gold. This failed, and he became a bear on stocks, especially on Western Union Telegraph stock. The reported earnings of the railroads were greatly in excess of those of the previous year, and yet the newspapers accused the directors of the Milwaukee & St. Paul railroad of depressing their stock in order to buy it. (A strangely familiar item.)

Money began to rise in price early in September, and

the reserve decreased. The week before the panic the reserve fell below legal requirement, and money on call on stock collateral commanded a premium above the legal rate. Sixty-day commercial paper was discounted at from nine to twelve per cent per annum. September 8, the New York Warehouse & Security' Co. was reported in trouble. This company had made considerable advances on bonds of new railroads. September 12, the firm of Kenyon, Cox & Co., in which Daniel Drew was a general partner, failed to meet its engagements, owing to endorsements of railroad paper, particularly the paper of the Canada Southern. September 15, Jay Cooke & Co. closed their doors, and the absolute tranquillity and confidence of less than thirty days previous was succeeded by the wildest agitation.

An account of the scene in Wall street on the days following the suspension of Jay Cooke & Co. and before the Stock Exchange closed its doors, describes "the brute terror with which great crowds of men rushed to and fro, trying to get rid of their property, almost begging people to take it from them at any price," and says, "No dog was ever so much alarmed by the clatter of the saucepan (at his heels) as hundreds seemed to be by the possession of really valuable and dividend-paying securities, and no horse was ever more reckless in extricating himself from the débris of a broken carriage than these swarms of acute and shrewd traders in divesting themselves of their possessions. Hundreds must really, to judge by their conduct, have been so confused by terror and anxiety as to be unable

to decide whether they desired to have or not have, to
be poor or rich.''

The interesting question to the calm observer, at this
distance of time, is as to the cause which could produce
such wild terror in men not different in any particular
respect from ourselves. Was it the sudden realization
that they had borrowed more than they could readily
pay, which drove them crazy? How was this change
in feeling brought about? During the previous summer there were numerous prophecies of impending
financial trouble. But this goes for nothing. There
are always plenty of such prophecies. No storm ever
sweeps the sky but some grumbler has foretold it, and
there is no day so bright, but it is marked for a cataclysm
in some calendar. There are always innumerable
signs of the times, which one notices afterward, and
there would be a panic every month in every year, if the
foretelling disaster could produce it. But no one of
the forebodings, which I have met with, has attempted
to show the special condition in which men's minds are
suddenly converted from a state of perfect confidence
to a state of absolute fear. It is not credible that
men generally were so ignorant of their financial conditions in August, that an examination of their affairs
in September could throw them into despair. Yet it is
necessary to imagine such a situation, in order to
account for the effect produced. If we can suppose
that the clerks of the majority of the bankers of Wall
street had robbed their employers of half their capital

and absconded together, or if there had been a common falsification of accounts, we might find a sufficient reason for a general collapse of credit.   But no such treason or deception was charged or believed.

Could the panic have been averted if Jay Cooke & Co. had secured a loan sufficient to have met their current obligations?   Could the business of the country have been brought by wise management to a sound basis without a general liquidation?   Conjecture only can answer.

It is firmly implanted in our minds, because we have passed through the experience, that some such process of fright and sacrifice, of distrust and realization, is necessary occasionally to produce a sound state of credit. But the proposition will hardly bear examination.   Blind fear and unreasoning distrust should characterize only the ignorant and inexperienced.   Well trained men of affairs should never give way to such passions.   It is only by supposing that the business world is a mob of ill-taught and ill-informed novices, that we can imagine them liable to such affections.   It is known that raw levies and undrilled crowds can be panic-stricken by vague danger, but disciplined and skillful soldiers cannot be stampeded by uncertainties or sudden alarms. And, by this analogy, it may be asserted that when the business of the country is controlled by men of sound courage and good training, financial panics will be impossible.   It is not utopian to look for a time when financial catastrophe will be averted by organization— when threatened congestion of prices will be prevented by scientific treatment. There are many philanthropists and statesmen who expect the time when wars will be avoided by international arbitration—

" When the common sense of most shall hold a fretful realm in awe,
And the kindly earth shall slumber lapt in universal law ; "

then the same common sense, which restrains angry passions, will check sudden fear; and when masses of men possess the self-control to submit their disputes to the decision of disinterested tribunals, they can no longer be stampeded in blind terror by any unexpected event, whether financial or physical.

I have said that no panic is a repetition of any other, and I think that an examination of the history of financial affairs will show that the special causes which have led up to each panic have been removed in the time following. Each panic has had its lesson, which has been practically learned.

The English people have not speculated wildly in railway shares since the time of Hudson, nor committed their funds blindly to limited liability companies since the failure of Overend, Gurney & Co., nor invested indiscriminately in the stocks of foreign states since the days of the Foreign Loans Committee.

In this country there has been no speculation in land as rabid as that immediately preceding 1837. We have thoroughly reformed our banking system, so that the "wild-cat scare of 1857" can never visit us again. I think also that we have learned wisdom from 1873, and are exercising great caution in the matter of loans. Mer-

3

chants and manufacturers generally are careful about increasing their liabilities beyond a fair proportion to their capital. And bankers are cautious in giving accommodations. There is but little disposition to borrow money on mortgage, or to buy real estate on partial payments. And although the amount of railroad bonds has greatly increased, and is increasing daily, yet, except on roads completed and in successful operation, these are scarcely salable at any price, and are not accepted as collateral. Before 1873 all the manufacturers of and dealers in railroad iron and equipment were burdened with bonds on partially constructed roads, on which they had made advances of goods or material. Now the rolling-mill companies and the car builders of the country have little or none of this species of property in their hands.

Business men have been taught by trial. They will not put themselves in positions which they have found may be so unpleasant. If panic comes again, it must find some new avenue of approach. It will not come at any appointed time, like an eclipse. We cannot make engagements for its appearance. Neither will it come in familiar form, so that we may know it when it approaches; nor by its old paths, so that we may guard against and resist it.

The only safe prophecies which we can make concerning it are, that if it comes it will come when we are not looking for it, and that it will be something different from what we have anticipated.

The assassination of President Garfield very nearly caused a panic, and did cause a very considerable liquidation of accounts. Startling and horrible as was the intelligence that the President of the United States had been suddenly shot and probably mortally wounded, there was nothing in the fact which should have disturbed the business of the country. But the shock to the sensibilities of men was so great that many ceased to reason, and acted from blind terror. If the tragedy had occurred on a day when all the exchanges were open and business was in full course, in all probability a severe panic would have occurred. But it was on Saturday, the 2d of July. The Chicago Board of Trade and other exchanges were not in session, and many business men were away from their offices for the coming holiday. The Stock Exchange in New York, however, was open, and simultaneously, as it seemed, with the flashing of the news over the land came the orders to sell stocks. Prices fell rapidly, and transactions became very large. It was nearly a panic, but a few men, who had great personal interests at stake, met together and gave orders to buy all of certain principal stocks which were offered at certain prices. By this means the panic was averted. The next day was Sunday, and on Monday, the 4th, all business was suspended in this country. But the Stock Exchange in London was to be feared, and the same men who had bought all stocks offered in New York on Saturday bought, also, in London on Monday, so that American securities were quoted steady in European markets, and

at the opening of the Stock Exchange in New York, on
Tuesday morning, there was no longer a pressure to sell,
and stocks advanced.

But although an actual panic was prevented, some of
the consequences of panic followed. The nerves of
the American business public seem to have been badly
shaken. General despondency took the place of sanguine expectation. As the life of the President slowly
ebbed away, the vigor of great enterprises and the anima-
tion of trade seemed to depart. A gradual decline in
prices set in, which, perhaps, has not yet reached its
turning point; and many a man can now see that the
bullet of Guiteau shattered his chance of fortune, and
not a few date from that crazy deed their financial ruin.

As most of the men now in business remember vivid-
ly the panic of 1873, and believe that it was made possible by an unwise expansion of credit,—that is, that
nearly everyone had borrowed more money than the
capital employed in his business would warrant,—so
most men expect to avert the consequences of the next
panic from themselves by caution in the matter of loans.

It may be admitted that a panic can hardly cause continuous and widespread disaster where there is no great
indebtedness; yet I think that a panic may occur and
a distressing decline in prices follow, even when there is
no unwise extension of credits. Debts were not greater
than they should be at the time of the assassination of
Garfield, yet we barely escaped a panic, and experienced
a very unpleasant fall in prices.

It is well, therefore, to take notice that there are other causes of panic than unwise borrowing and lending, and to be on our guard against other dangers which may menace our commercial prosperity.

There is danger of panic in any cause which may depress prices. Hopefulness naturally is a continuous force, while despondency acts spasmodically. Hopefulness is pleasant, and we encourage it to remain. Despondency is unpleasant, and we admit it only when it is forced upon us. The tendency to higher prices is agreeable, but the tendency to lower prices is disagreeable, and we yield to it reluctantly. If we could divest ourselves of feeling, and look at prices only as reasoning beings, we should accept a fall in prices when the state of trade favored it, and there would be no panics. Gradually by the development of knowledge and training we may approach this condition. We or our descendants may have the ability to balance cause and effect dispassionately, and the wisdom and self-sacrifice to accept lower prices contentedly. It is true that the professional speculator cultivates this quality, and the short seller (of whom I have more to say later) may be the germ from which the future masters of commerce will develop.

There are now dimly descernible on our horizon several scarecrows which, some time in the twilight when we are off guard, may be metamorphosed into active spooks and throw us into spasms of fright.

There is demagogism,—the efforts of many editors

and politicians to create and arouse prejudice in the
people against the machinery of commerce.   It is a
common thing to hear the men most prominent in or-
ganizing industries and developing the wealth and
resources of the country, denounced as monopolists and
robbers, or to see in the columns of leading newspapers
those admirable devices for public benefit, the railroad
companies and the banks, styled swindling schemes or
frauds upon the rights of men.   We have become so
used to this rant that it fails to make us indignant.
We know the editors and the politicians do not mean
what they say, and we fall into the belief that no one is
deluded by them.   But none the less is this a real danger.   This constant demagogic raving serves to keep
these absurd prejudices alive, and events may occur
which will cause them to flame up with disastrous vio-
lence.

The danger with which demagogism menaces us most
visibly just now is the silver dollar.   The government
is adding two millions per month to its hoard of these
coins, which are useless in trade with the world.   If we
have a season of depressed prices, and of complaints from
the people, will not this depreciated currency be forced
into circulation?   If this comes suddenly it will create
a panic of capital anxious to escape out of the country
and take itself in the form of gold over the sea.   If it
comes gradually it will have the same effect, only the
country will grow poorer more slowly.

The danger of demagogism against the banks and in
reference to legal tender paper money has probably

passed for the present, but no one can tell when it will break out again.

Against railroad companies demagogues find a constant exercise of their voices. But, by a sort of inertia, the railroads seem to be able to ward off the damage which all sorts of absurd laws threaten to inflict upon them, until a general notion prevails that the railroads can defy demagogues — and also the rest of the people. Indeed the bills and enactments of legislatures, on this subject, are generally regarded as nothing more than invitations from the demagogues to the railroad men to come and corrupt them.

There is little danger of a financial panic in this country from the immediate actions of socialists, communists, nihilists, or the liberators of Ireland by dynamite. There is no mark in this country sufficiently prominent to draw their sensation-seeking fire. The peculiar glory which they covet can hardly be gained by ruining our public buildings or slaughtering a score of congressmen. But the destruction which they may cause in Europe may react with disastrous effect upon our trade and prosperity.

Whatever combination of circumstances tends to a serious depression of prices may produce a panic, if not well understood and wisely accepted. But the danger of panic is much increased, if prices are artificially sustained when they should naturally fall.

I think there are three ways in which there is danger

that prices will be artificially sustained when they would
naturally decline, and by such artificial support the very
matter and form of panic may be provided:

First, the price of labor. It is sought by combinations among the employed in every branch of trade and
manufactures to raise the compensation of labor to the
highest possible point. These combinations,—trades
unions, brotherhoods or knights of labor—are very well
if managed with caution and sagacity. But the difficulty just now is that workmen are inexperienced in
managing these combinations. They have a greatly
exaggerated idea of their importance and power. They
are determined to exact the last cent which employers
can be induced to pay, and to refuse to work and to
prevent others working, if they can't get it. As a consequence, the largest part of the manufacturing of the
country is now carried on on a very light margin of
profit, if not at a positive loss. A slight fall in prices
would make manufacturing generally a losing under-
taking, unless a corresponding reduction in wages could
be effected. This, if we may judge from the present
temper of the combinations, would not be agreed to.
What is true of manufacturing is true of building and
mining and railroad operating, and of most of the forms
of production (except farming) in which labor is employed.

This condition of affairs is aggravated by a large immigration of laborers from Europe. The natural effect
of this immigration would be to stimulate manufacturing by providing cheaper labor. Under the control

of the combinations, however, the rate of wages is sustained, and manufacturing and other forms of production are barely maintaining average activity. The result of this state of affairs, especially if there is a fall in prices of manufactured goods, may be a panic among manufacturers—a general rush to withdraw capital from such unprofitable investments.

Second, the prices of railroad stocks and bonds may be artificially sustained, above their natural level, so persistently, that a sudden and ruinous break may be caused by the sheer force of financial gravity. On the first of January, 1879, there were in operation in the United States about 81,000 miles of railroads. It is estimated that there are now in operation about 115,000 miles. There has been an addition of 42 per cent to the railroad mileage in four years. This is an enormous increase, and greater than the increase of the industries of the country in any other direction. The cost of these railroads has been taken from the surplus profits of the country, or from its floating capital. Have the people of this country earned this money, over and above their cost of living, as fast as the railroad builders have spent it? It seems impossible that they could have done so, and, if not, it has been taken from the floating capital. That is, we probably have put more into fixtures than we can afford to. We see sometimes a too sanguine merchant building a store so large that with his remaining capital he cannot fill it with goods, or a manufacturer providing himself such an extensive

plant that he cannot operate it to advantage.   It may
be that, as a people, we are in the same condition.   If
this is our case, the prices of railroad stocks and bonds
should be such as, at least, not to encourage further
expenditure in that direction.

But the conditions under which the prices of the railroad stocks and bonds are made are peculiar.   The
facility with which investments can be made in these
securities and the ease with which they can be realized
upon are so great, that they draw a large proportion of
the free capital of the country.   The machinery of the
Stock Exchange is well devised and smoothly operated.
Any one who wishes to make an investment has a long
list of stocks and bonds to choose from.   He has but to
say a word and the particular security he wants is bought.
He pays for it and it is delivered to him, or if he wishes
to pay only a part of the price, his broker, without any
trouble to his customer, borrows the balance of the purchase price and the customer is at liberty to complete
the transaction at any time.   The purchaser has no an-
noyance with details, as he would in buying a house or a
farm, a factory or a mine, or in lending on mortgage or
on commercial paper.   And likewise, if one wishes to
sell any of the securities quoted on the New York Stock
Exchange, he only gives the order and his property is
sold.   It is delivered and paid for without a word.
There is no other kind of property which can be sold
and transferred with half this readiness and regularity.
The quickness and precision with which this machinery
of exchange is worked attracts capital and encourages

speculation. As a consequence, a considerable part of the capital in railroads is invested with the expectation of deriving profit, not from the earnings of the property, but from the rise in price of the stock. The result is a large and powerful influence, constantly at work, to maintain a rising scale in prices. This influence exerts itself in many ways with extraordinary shrewdness and perseverance, — in the publication of favorable rumors, in exaggerating earnings and concealing expenses, in the formation of pools to sustain prices, and in a thousand devices which cannot be detected or described.

The danger is that these methods may be pursued too long and too successfully, and that some day they may be discovered to be deceptions, and a rush to sell all railroad investments may follow.

Fortunately there are bears. In the ingenious machinery of the Stock Exchange it is arranged that stocks and bonds may be borrowed readily, and so any one who thinks any of this property is selling at a higher price than it is worth, may borrow it and sell it. This is " selling short," and the seller is generally able to borrow the stock, which he has sold, for an indefinite period. Of course he must finally buy the stock and make a return of that which he borrowed. But so quickly and easily is this process performed by the brokers, that it is usually no more trouble to sell stocks before buying to make a profit on the decline, than it is to buy before selling to make profit on the rise. Thus bears are provided, speculators who operate for a fall.

And very useful members of the commercial commu-
nity are these bears, although they are visited with
much abuse and little sympathy.   They are few in
number compared with the bulls—the sanguine speculators for a rise—and they have comparatively little
capital with which to back their ventures.   They are
usually hard-headed men who care nothing for popu-
larity, but have a great regard for facts.   They are in-
credulous as to rumors, suspicious as to official state-
ments, and accept affidavits with caution.   They are
doomed to pass long periods in moodiness and neglect,
while the sanguine crowd is exulting in rising prices,
and when prices fall and they grimly take their gains,
they are looked upon by the majority as the prophets
and contrivers of all their woes.

The bears do much to prevent prices rising much
above their natural level in the stock market, but they
are at best only spasmodic operators, and have not the
same permanent interest in the prices of railroad properties that the bulls have.   Having capital and numbers on their side, it is highly probable that the bulls will
succeed in forcing prices up to a dangerously high
point, from which they may come tumbling down, when
we suddenly discover that we have put too much of our
floating capital into railroad building.

Third, corners are the means of creating artificially
high prices, and preparing the market for panic and
general collapse.

. Causing high prices of breadstuffs by manipulation

has always been reckoned shameful, and has been an
offense against law in all countries, civilized and un-
civilized. Forestalling, buying a commodity on its
way to market with a view to enhance its price, en-
grossing, buying all or nearly all of a commodity in
the market, regrating, buying corn or provisions with
the view of selling at a higher price in the same or a
neighboring market,— all mild forms of cornering were
offenses at common law, and were punished by the pil-
lory, by loss of property or by imprisonment. The
Roman law also punished dealers for these practices, and
for other misdemeanors calculated to raise the price of
provisions. This is also a crime in Oriental lands. No
longer ago than April, 1881, the Prince-Governor of
Karman, in Persia, cut off the ears and plucked out
the beard of a baker, who succeeded in cornering the
grain market of Karman.

This is also nominally forbidden by the statutes 'of
Illinois ; but the laws of Illinois are less carefully
enforced than those of Persia. There is a successful
corner in some kind of grain or provisions nearly every
month in Illinois, and no one is ever punished there-
for, except the rash men who expect that the law will
be enforced.

The use of the word "corner" in this sense is an
American invention, and its sense seems to be misap-
prehended in England. Bagehot, while saying that it
is an American "cant word," defined it to mean a
"gang of persons who obtain possession of the whole
supply of any article, and will only sell·at an excessive

price." The chief dictionary in use in England says a "corner" is "a clique or party formed to take posses-sion, &c." This is not a correct definition. The gang, clique or party engaged in cornering the market for any commodity are not spoken of as the corner. Mr. C. F. Adams, Jr., is nearer right in defining it as "the result produced by a combination of persons who, while secretly holding the whole or the greater part of any stock or species of property, induce another com-bination to agree to deliver them a large further quantity at some future time." But it is not necessary that there should be a combination of persons, or that the managers of the corner should first secretly hold the whole or a large part of any commodity, or that the agreements to deliver a further quantity should be induced by them. A corner, according to our under-standing, is that condition of the market for any com-modity, when one person or party holds all of the commodity in that market and also holds contracts for the delivery of a considerable quantity more. The object of creating a corner is to compel those who have contracted to deliver the commodity to pay an exor-bitant price for it.

The public has two standpoints from which it regards corners, especially corners in grain or provisions, and it depends on its temper at the time which view it takes.

In times of adversity, when trade is dull and profits are small and wages are low, and the closest economy in means of living is necessary, then a corner in pro-

visions is felt as a tax on each man's bread. Then it is
regarded as forestalling was regarded in the days of the
Henrys and the Edwards, as an offense against public
trade which must be suppressed and punished. Then
the public denounces corners, and the legislature makes
laws against them. But when matters are more prosperous, when wages are fair and everyone has enough to
eat, and there is little anxiety as to the future, then the
farmers rejoice in the high prices of wheat or corn or
pork or lard, although they have sold what they have
had, they have more coming on, and it is not easy to
make the prices seem exorbitant to them. Then the
spirit of speculation is abroad in the land, and there is
a sympathy with and a gratification at higher prices;
then there is scorn for the men who "sell what they
haven't got," and a satisfaction in making them pay
roundly for their temerity. Looking from this standpoint the public approves corners, and the law, which
the legislature has placed on the statute-book against
them, is a dead letter.

It is, however, as they create artificial prices that I
wish especially to call attention to corners. It is the
general testimony of experts in cornering markets, that
with few exceptions corners are unprofitable to those
engaged in them. It is almost impossible to sell the
commodity after the corner is completed for enough to
cover first cost, and frequently the loss in marketing the
stock which has accumulated is greater than the amount
which has been squeezed from the shorts. A corner in

any prominent article of commerce, such as grain or cotton, deranges the course of trade and makes subsequent prices irregular and uncertain. The effect of the great corner in wheat in 1879 and 1880 was the suspension of exports of this product to Europe, the reduction of ocean rates to nominal figures, the driving of many vessels from New York to foreign ports and the opening of the wheat export trade of Calcutta. This was a permanent damage to the productive industries of this country. It happened that this corner was thoroughly carried to its legitimate conclusion. It was not a mere conspiracy to squeeze a few shorts. The syndicate, who bought nearly all the wheat in the country, seemed to have believed that Europe must have it at any price, and they looked for a large profit in selling it for actual consumption. But they were greatly in error. They found that the world could get on for awhile without their wheat, and they were at last willing to close out their speculation at a considerable loss.

The influence which this great corner exercised on the wheat trade of the world, the lesser corners, which are at times almost of monthly occurrence on the Chicago Board of Trade, exercise also, only in a less marked manner. They demoralized trade and create fictitious prices.

Much has been said in the newspapers about the corner in spring wheat in July 1882. This corner was successful, as corners go. The shorts were forced to settle their contracts, after a prolonged and stubborn contest, at prices greatly beyond what the property could be sold for, for actual consumption. And yet the accounts of the corner, if they are settled, cannot show any very satisfactory result. There were about 16,000,-000 bushels of spring wheat bought by the clique at prices not varying far from 1.25. Of this, 6,000,000 bushels were delivered, being all the No. 2 spring wheat in the Chicago elevators, and on 10,000,000 bushels the difference between 1.25 and 1.35 (the settling price fixed by the committee) was paid, amounting to about $1,000,-000. But the clique were obliged to sell the 6,000,000 bushels of wheat, which they had on hand, to consumers. The greater part was exported. It could not have been sold at prices equal to one dollar per bushel in Chicago, and much of it undoubtedly went for less. However, if we reckon the 6,000,000 bushels sold at one dollar per bushel, there is a loss to the clique of $1,500,000, which is partly paid by the $1,000,000 squeezed from the shorts, leaving as net cost to the clique, for the pleasure and excitement of cornering the market, $500,000.

If the clique and the shorts together lost $1,500,000, who gained it? Undoubtedly a large part of this sum went to the producers of the wheat. The farmers or their agents realized twenty-five cents per bushel more for this 6,000,000 bushels, than they would if it had been sold directly to the consumer, and had not been cornered on the way.

And yet, in the long run, perhaps the farmers are greatest losers from corners. For the artificial prices created by corners give them extravagant ideas of the

4

value of their produce, lead them to look not to legitimate demand but to manipulation of the market for
their profit, and tend to form for their calculations
unreal and unsafe bases.

It is not, perhaps, possible for a financial panic to be
directly caused by a corner, or a series of corners, in
grain or provisions, as matters are at present conducted
in our exchanges.   But it is hardly possible to overlook
the danger in these periodically inflated prices. As long
as the speculators alone suffer, the public may be careless,
and the farmers may chuckle and approve.   But some
day one of these corners will squeeze the consumers
perceptibly.   Already it is asserted that the high price
at which American corn is held is stimulating production
in new fields.   Some day we may find that, with a large
supply of breadstuff in the country, there is much suffer-
ing among the poorer people, and inability in Europe to
pay our prices.   And then we may find that European
markets are filled with other grain, and that ours is not
wanted.   If such a condition of our trade were rapidly
brought about, it would undoubtedly cause a most
destructive panic and fall in prices.

Bagehot has expressed the opinion that a rise in prices
is started by some large profit in some trade or line of
production.   The people engaged in this line find that
they are accumulating a surplus, and have something
more to spend.   This stimulates production in other

trades, and gradually the whole commercial world is filled with confidence and a belief in higher prices.

It seems to me that the downward movement is produced in a similar way by a great loss in any trade or line of production. This loss should cause a curtailment of expenditure, less activity in trade, a lessening of confidence, and a belief in lower prices.

If this view is correct, it is the part of intelligence to see the fact when it exists, and the part of wisdom to accept the legitimate consequences cheerfully. We cannot always be blessed with rising prices. Sometimes the tendency must be in the opposite direction. Declining prices are not necessarily caused by folly, carelessness or wickedness. They cannot be prevented by wisdom, diligence and righteousness. Declining prices are not disgraceful, and may not even indicate a general cessation of prosperity. Periods of declining prices are marked by careful accounting, by closer criticism of business methods, by diminished waste, by the better adapting of means to ends. In such periods invention is stimulated and good habits are strengthened.

But declining prices do not imply congested prices. Seasons of declining prices must come, but panics may be avoided. We are just now probably in a period of declining prices. There has been a great fall in the price of iron, and a great curtailment of profit in that trade. It is inevitable, if the theory here described is correct, that this loss should spread to other trades and lines of production and result in a lessened demand for all commodities and a general fall in prices. If the commercial world accepts this inevitable decline calmly and intelligently, and judiciously provides for it, its consequences may be strengthened credit, better organized machinery of trade, a broader and safer basis for future production. But if it is resisted by the various means I have indicated, it is possible that panic and all the disastrous consequences may be imminent. If demagogues endeavor to sustain prices by meddling with the currency or attacking the railroads; if the combinations of laborers maintain artificial prices for labor, or the combinations of capitalists artificial prices for stocks and securities, or the combinations of speculators artificial prices for grain, provisions and other commodities, the whole falsehood will some day be suddenly and generally recognized. Then prices will come down with a run, in a state of violent and painful congestion, and the consequences it will require years to realize.

May 7, 1883.

Milton Keynes UK
Ingram Content Group UK Ltd.
UKHW040931180224
437992UK00003B/167